An Australian
1,2,3
of Animals

Little Hare Books
an imprint of
Hardie Grant Egmont
85 High Street
Prahran, Victoria 3181, Australia
www.littleharebooks.com

First published 2007
First published in paperback 2009
Reprinted 2009 (twice)
Reprinted 2010

National Library of Australia
Cataloguing-in-Publication entry

Bancroft, Bronwyn.

An Australian 1,2,3 of animals/Bronwyn Bancroft.

9781921272851 (pbk.)

For pre-school age.
Animals- -Australia- -Juvenile literature- -Pictorial works.
Counting- -Juvenile literature- -Pictorial works.

513.211

Designed by Serious Business
Additional designs by Bernadette Gethings
Produced by Pica Digital, Singapore
Printed through Phoenix Offset
Printed in Shenzhen, Guangdong Province, China, June 2010

8 7 6 5 4

An Australian 1, 2, 3 of Animals

Bronwyn Bancroft

LITTLE HARE

www.littleharebooks.com

*Dedicated to the advancement of equal
learning opportunities for all people.
And to my Mum and Rubyrose,
spanning the years with maths
—BB*

1

One platypus diving.

2

Two brolgas dancing.

3

Three koalas dozing.

4

Four crocodiles snapping.

5

Five kookaburras laughing.

Six sugar gliders sailing.

7

Seven turtles plodding.

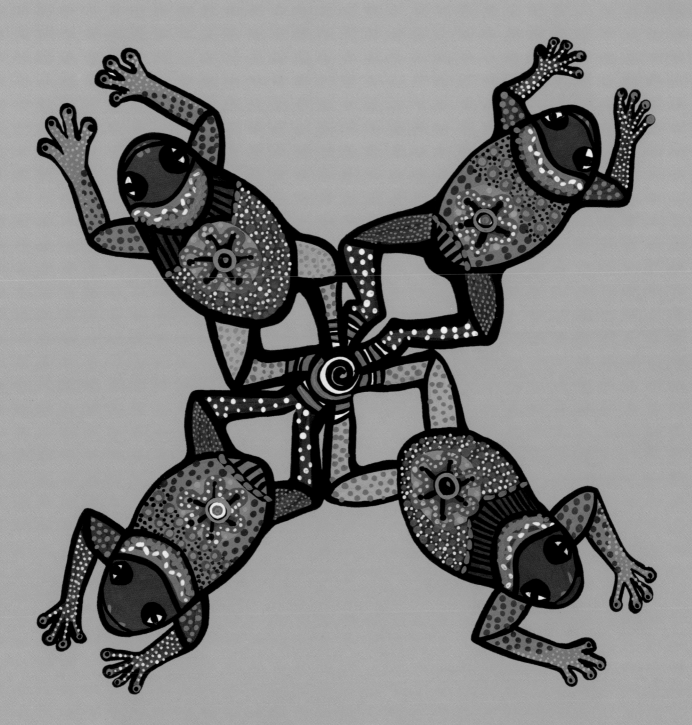

Eight frogs leaping.

Nine lizards hissing.

10

Ten ducks gliding.

11

Eleven geckos climbing.

12

Twelve emus running.

Thirteen galahs playing.

Fourteen wallabies hopping.

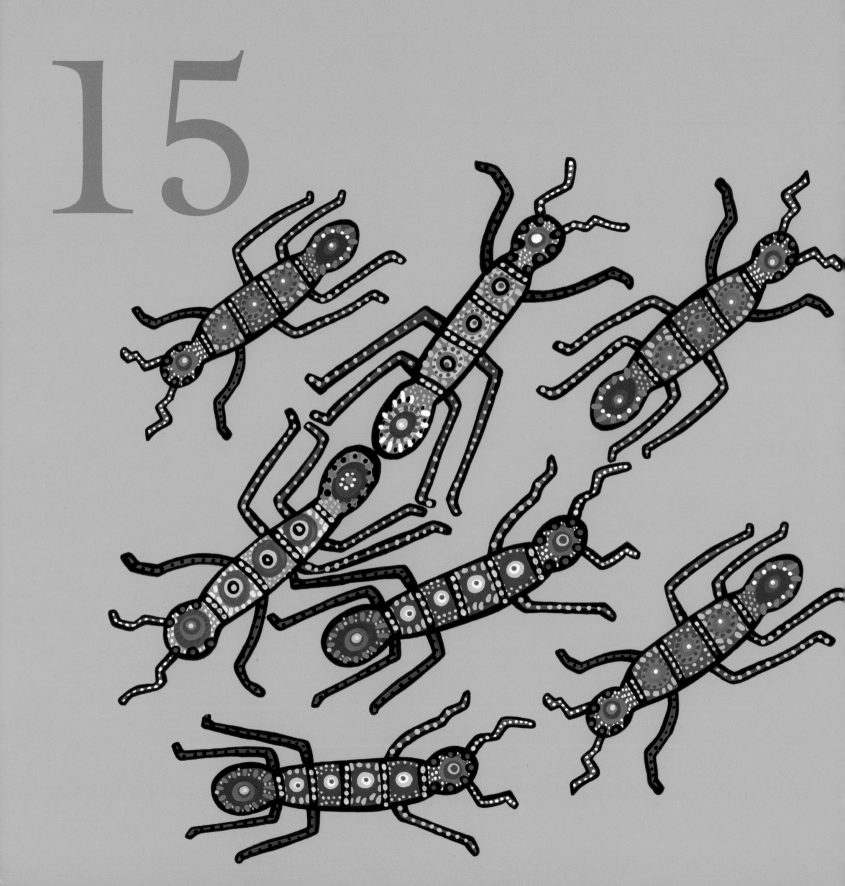

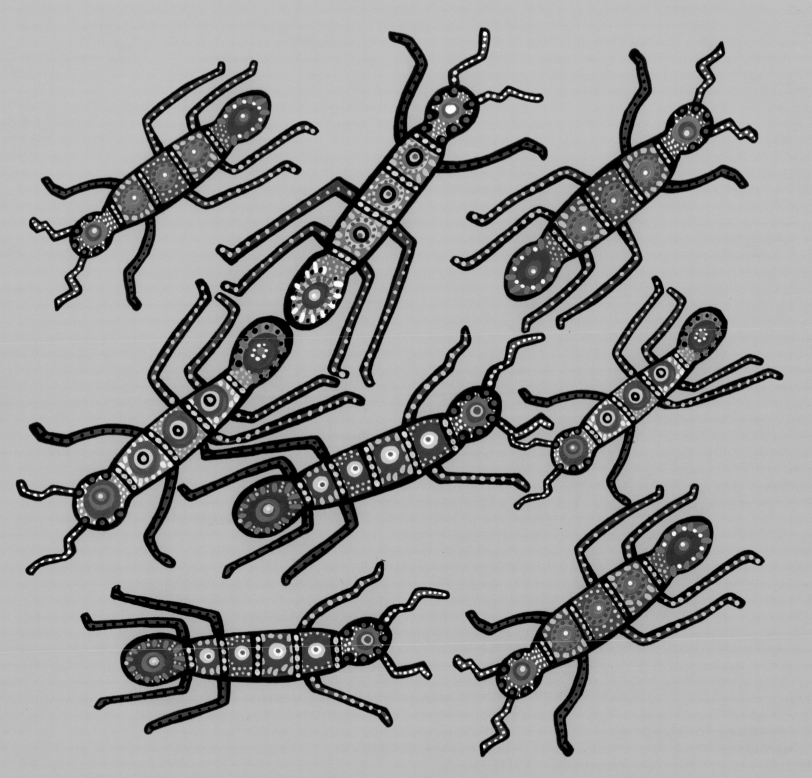

Fifteen bull ants swarming.

I am a descendant of the Bundjalung people.
The Bundjalung nation stretches from northern New South Wales
(which is where I grew up) to south-eastern Queensland. The paintings
in this book are a personal journey inside myself, an exploration in line
and colour. My artwork is not traditional, but when you are an
Aboriginal artist, you're not 'just' an artist—
you're a teacher, a facilitator. Although I live and work in the city now,
I know that my artistic talent descends from my Old People—
they have gifted it to me—and I feel very honoured by that.

Bronwyn Bancroft is an artist and designer whose artworks
have been collected and shown by galleries throughout Australia
and around the world. Since 1993 Bronwyn has
illustrated several award-winning children's books,
including *Fat and Juicy Place* (by Diana Kidd), *Big Rain Coming*
(by Katrina Germein), and Oodgeroo's *Stradbroke Dreamtime*.

Bronwyn lives in Sydney with her children Jack, Ella and Rubyrose.